For parents who pause at bedtime, searching for the right words to tell the story of how your family came to be—your stories matter. Let's celebrate the beautiful, messy journey of parenthood together!

It was a Sunday,
bright and clear.
Pia woke up,
smiling ear to ear.

**She felt cheerful,
happy and bright,**

**Grateful for her world ...
the love and light.**

**But when the day ended,
stars came out,**

**Pia's smile turned
into a pout.**

There was a hole in her heart.
Often, it felt like it might fall apart.

Her doctor was very clear,
'Your heart has a missing
piece, my dear.'

So, Pia did what she knew best,
She put on her bravest face and began her quest.

On land ...

Under the sea ...

Up in the sky,
as high as can be.

She followed her heart, with hope and cheer,
But the missing piece was still not near.

Finally, as she travelled near and far,

The answer sparkled like a star.

She knew what would fill her heart.
A little daughter. A fresh start.

The doctor said, 'There is a special place, where babies stay, till a parent takes them home one day.'

In her heart,
Pia knew this was true.
Her search had ended
with the perfect clue.

Pia dashed to the home,
in a flash and a bound.
It was filled with the cutest kids
and a few grown-ups around.

She saw a little girl with hair so wild,
Deep dimples that made her heart smile.
She heard a voice out of the blue,
She's the one—the one for you!

Her search ended at last …
She had found *her perfect match!*

Her search ended at last …
She had found *her*
perfect match!

**And when she walked in,
smelling of strawberries.
Aye's heart danced,
bursting with joy so merry.**

Aye waited—happily,
full of hope, indeed.
For the perfect match
for her bedtime read.

And then one day,
there was a buzz in the air.
Whispers said—a lady
was on her way, just for Aye!

She just knew,
Her time had come, too.

Always a little drama star,
Aye shouted, *'My mamma is not far!'*

She saw her friends go, hand in hand,
With a mum or dad, feeling so glad.

A mamma bird feeding her little one ...

A goldfish and mamma, having lots of fun.

Everything felt right,
with love so true,
Aye's search ended,
with the perfect clue.

But then she saw something
sweet and warm,
A kitten cuddled with her mamma,
safe from harm.

Nope, not there.
That’s not fair

But Aye wanted to
know some more,
She searched for the
answer high and low.

She popped a balloon,
but it wasn't inside,
Not under the train or
the trees so wide.

The doctor said with a thoughtful frown,
'It looks like a broken heart, hands down'.

But something didn't feel quite right,
Aye searched for it with all her might.
She often wondered what could it be,
That hidden thing she couldn't see.

She lived in a house
full of kids and noise,
A pet cat. A red balloon
and few toys.

The happiest little girl,
With the cutest smile
in the world.

It was a bright, sunny Sunday.
Aye woke up smiling, ready to play.

Preeta Sukhtankar is a passionate storyteller who has worn many hats—journalist, television producer, start-up founder, and now a dedicated advisor to female entrepreneurs. An adoptive parent, she lives in Mumbai in a happy home filled with art, alongside her talkative and creative daughter. Preeta is excited to return to her first love—writing—with her debut book, a heartfelt love letter to her child.

Published by Red Panda, an imprint of Westland Books, a division of Nasadiya Technologies Private Limited, in 2024

No. 269/2B, First Floor, 'Irai Arul', Vimalraj Street, Nethaji Nagar, Alapakkam Main Road, Maduravoyal, Chennai 600095

Westland, the Westland logo, Red Panda and the Red Panda logo are the trademarks of Nasadiya Technologies Private Limited, or its affiliates.

Visual art direction: Radhika Chopra

ISBN: 9789360453015

10 9 8 7 6 5 4 3 2 1

Royalties accrued from the sale of this book will go to Bal Asha Trust (www.balashatrust.org)

Printed at Nutech Print Services, India